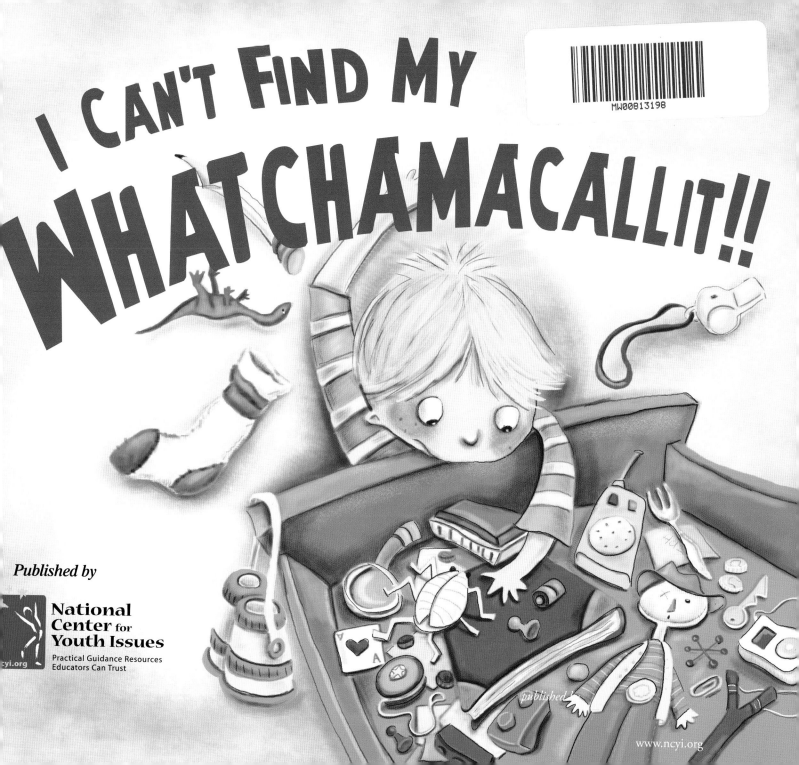

I CAN'T FIND MY WHATCHAMACALLIT!!

Published by

National Center for Youth Issues

Practical Guidance Resources
Educators Can Trust

ncyi.org

www.ncyi.org

To the person in the mirror!
– Julia

Duplication and Copyright

No part of this publication may be reproduced, stored in a retrieval system or transmitted in any form by any means, electronic, mechanical, photocopy, recording or otherwise without prior written permission from the publisher except for all worksheets and activities which may be reproduced for a specific group or class. Reproduction for an entire school or school district is prohibited.

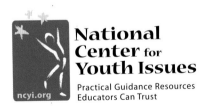

National Center for Youth Issues
Practical Guidance Resources
Educators Can Trust
ncyi.org

P.O. Box 22185
Chattanooga, TN 37422-2185
423.899.5714 • 800.477.8277
fax: 423.899.4547 • www.ncyi.org

ISBN: 978-1-937870-38-6
© 2015 National Center for Youth Issues, Chattanooga, TN
All rights reserved.
Written by: Julia Cook
Illustrations by: Michelle Hazelwood Hyde
Design by: Phillip W. Rodgers
Contributing Editor: Beth Spencer Rabon
Published by National Center for Youth Issues • Softcover
Printed at Starkey Printing, Chattanooga, Tennessee, U.S.A., October 2015

My name is Cletus.

Sometimes, I have a hard time keeping track of all my whatchamacallits (that's code word for stuff.)

3

"Cletus… Why did you choose not to comb your hair?"

"I couldn't find my comb."

"Cletus… Where is your homework?"

"I remember doing it, but I can't remember where I put it!"

"Cletus…Where is your other gym shoe?"

"I could only find one."

"Cletus… How come you didn't come to our soccer game last night?"

"We had a game?"

Bocephus is my cousin. He lives down the street. He's a neat freak!!! He's probably the most organized person on the planet! But if he ever loses anything, it **TOTALLY** freaks him out!

Bocephus always says:

"There's a home for everything! Every whatchamacallit has a spot. When you take something out, just put it back. I'm organized...Cletus, you're not!"

One time, Bocephus lost his slingshot,
and he **TOTALLY** freaked out!

"I NEVER lose my stuff! he screeched.
I'm as organized as can be!
It was right here, and now it's gone!
This CAN'T be happening to me!"

"Chill out Bocephus. We'll find your slingshot.

It couldn't have gone very far.

Why can't you be more like Cletus,

instead of the way that you are?"

Turns out, the dog ate Bocephus'
slingshot...well most of it!

Today, we're having a neighborhood garage sale. Every year my mom lets me sell my old toys, and then I get to keep the money and buy new toys.

Yesterday after school, my mom said, "Clean your room, Cletus, so you can decide what you want to sell this year."

I was going to sell my racetrack...

but I couldn't find the whatchamacallits that hook it all together.

I was going to sell my old remote control truck...

but I couldn't find the remote that makes it go.

I was going to sell my paint set...

but then I changed my mind.
Besides, I couldn't find the paintbrush that goes with it.

I was going to sell my soccer ball...

but it was flat, and I couldn't find the whatchamacallit to pump it up. Nobody wants to buy a flat soccer ball.

I was going to sell my hockey goalie gloves...

but I could only find one of them.

After the yard sale, Bocephus
came to my house to play.

"Cletus... do you remember what today is?"
my mom asked.

"It's Saturday," I answered.

"Yes and today is the day you are going to clean your room,
since you didn't get it done yesterday."

"Cletus!...you need to be more organized.
Your room is just a mess!
Your teacher called about your missing assignments.
There's 8 or 9, I guess.

In order to do well in life,
You need to be aware of three things...
Your brain, your body, and your stuff,
and you can't keep track of a thing!"

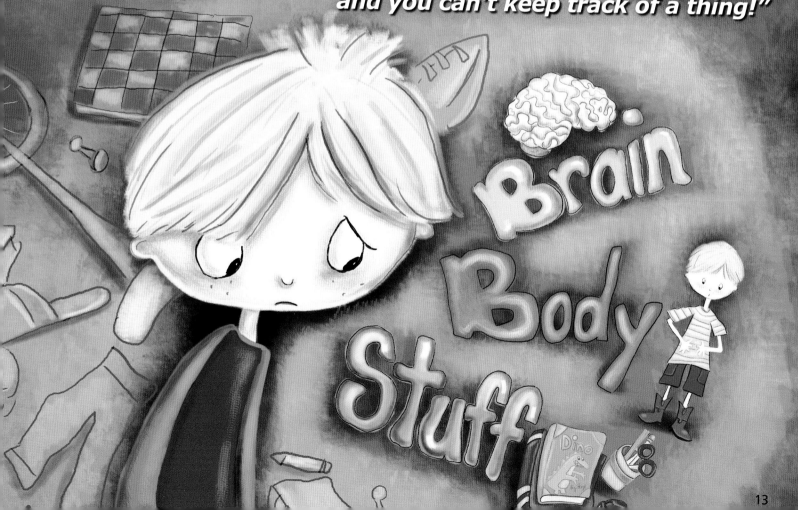

About an hour later,
Bocephus came to our door
with a bunch of stuff.

He had containers of all different sizes,

and an accordion folder with tabs,

Labels and a label maker,

and about 20 garbage bags!

14

"What's this stuff for?" I asked.

"You can't play until your room is clean, and at the rate you are going, you won't be able to play with me until next year!

So... I came here to help you clean it!"

"Where'd you get all this stuff?"

"I bought it with my yard sale money."

"Cletus...There's a home for everything.
Every whatchamacallit has its spot.
Let's sort through your stuff and put it where it goes.
I'm organized... Cletus, you're not!"

"Being organized doesn't mean you have to be a neat freak.

It just means that you can find whatever you are looking for in a reasonable amount of time...and in this big mess, you can't find anything!

First of all, we need to sort all of your stuff into 3 piles:"

KEEP ME

TOSS ME

GIVE ME AWAY

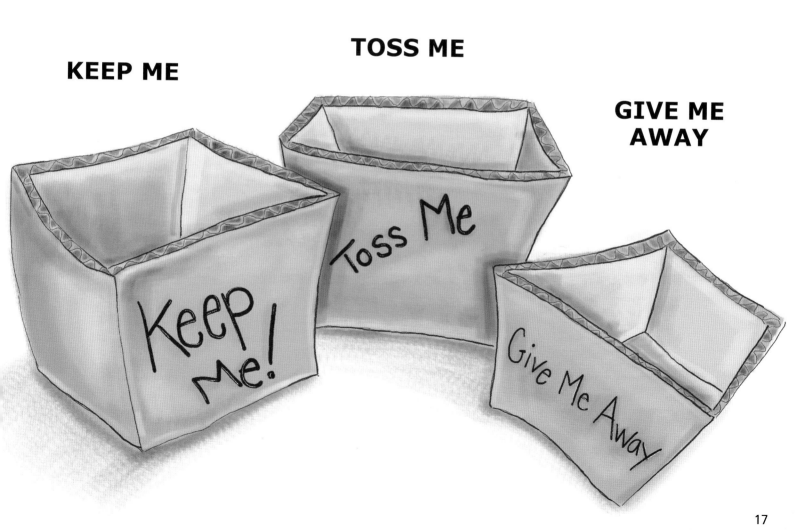

18

"That's easy!

Just ask yourself a few questions:

1. Is this thing adding to my life, or not?

2. Have I used it during the last year?

3. If I get rid of it, can I replace it if I need to?

4. Is there anyone else who might need it?"

Bocephus pulled out his label maker and started to make labels. Then he labeled all of the containers, and we started to sort.

We sorted, and sorted and sorted!
I couldn't believe what I found!

My racetrack whatchamacallits,
and my pump to make my ball round.

I found my missing assignments,
and even my remote control,

And a half-eaten bag of fruit snacks
that I was saving because I was full.

I even found my comb and my gym shoe
and the brush that goes with my paints.

My mom walked in when we were just about done,
and I thought she was going to faint!

The only thing that I could not find
was my other hockey glove.

We filled up 17 garbage bags.
We worked hard...me and my cuz!

Bocephus hung my calendar up on my bulletin board.
"Now maybe you won't miss another soccer game," he said.

"Now there's a home for everything.
All your whatchamacallits have their own spots.
When you get something out, just put it back.
See...organization ROCKS!

Now let's go play!"

"But what do I do with this?"

"That's an accordion folder. All of your school papers go in it. There's a section for every subject, but if you don't have time to put it in the right section, just throw it in there somewhere. Then you won't ever lose your assignments."

The next morning,
I went to get
Bocephus so we
could walk to school.
He was freaking out
again. He couldn't
find his book report.

"I NEVER lose my stuff!" He screeched

I'm as organized as can be!

It was right here, and now it's gone!

This CAN'T be happening to me!"

"Why didn't you put it into your
accordion folder?" I asked.

Then, I got an idea!

I had leftover stuff in my room from my diorama book report, and I knew exactly where it was.

So I ran to my house as fast as I could and grabbed everything Bocephus would need to build another diorama book report.

"I'm not creative enough to make a diorama! I can only do written book reports. How will I know where to glue all of this stuff?"

"That's easy! I said. I'll help you figure it out."

28

Bocephus got his diorama done really fast, and we made it to school just as the bell rang.

I helped Bocephus, and he helped me.
Now I'm as organized as can be!
Every whatchamacallit has its own special spot.
It's true... being organized really does ROCK!

Tips For Teaching Kids Organization Skills

Organization is an essential skill for people of all ages. As the educational demands of school-age children continue to increase, being more organized becomes vital for success. In fact, studies show that there is a direct correlation between academic achievement and organization. Having the organizational skills that are necessary for life-long success and productivity is invaluable! A child who possesses effective organizational skills can learn to manage not only daily responsibilities, but can also demonstrate the ability to plan ahead. Teaching a child to understand and apply organizational skills, however, can be tricky.

Here are a few tips that might help:

1. In order to buy into the concept of getting and staying organized, children need to understand its importance. Convince your child to learn organizational skills by explaining the benefits (i.e. less time spent doing homework and chores, more free time, less parental nagging, etc.) In order to do well at anything, children need to be in control of three things: their **BRAIN**, their **BODY**, and their **STUFF**. Having good organizational skills help to make that possible.

2. Maintain a positive outlook for being organized. Avoid having your child view organization as a punishment. Being more organized should always add to your child's life, not take from it.

3. Work with your child to develop a customized daily schedule that organizes activities, homework, play time, free time, mealtime, and bedtime. Some kids do best if they do their homework right after school, others need a break after school to play and/or unwind. **The more involved your child is in creating the schedule, the more likely he/she will follow it.** Display your child's schedule in a central location in his/her room.

4. Teach your child to make a daily checklist and celebrate when all entries are checked off.

5. Work with your child to break down large ongoing assignments and/or projects into smaller, more achievable tasks. The more involved your child is in planning this breakdown, the more likely he/she will be able to accomplish each task.

6. Invest in a family planning calendar so that your child realizes that others have commitments, too.

7. Have your child prepare for the next day before going to bed (i.e. lay clothes, shoes, boots, gloves out, put all homework and needed school items inside backpack and place backpack by the door, pack a lunch and put it in the fridge, etc.)

8. Let your child pick out an accordion folder at the store to be used for all school papers and homework assignments. Label each subject inside and encourage your child to file papers in the proper slot. If your child is in too much of a hurry to find the right slot, have him place the paper at the front of the folder and re-file it later. This way, all school papers end up going in one place. Encourage your child to organize his/her folder on a daily basis so that effective communication with school stays intact.

9. Create a homework supply box filled with supplies your child will need to do his/her homework (calculator, colored pencils, markers, scissors, glue, paper, etc.)

10. Designate a functional, consistent spot in your house to do homework.

11. Encourage your child to reorganize his/her room often using **KEEP**, **TOSS** and **DONATE** organizational bins.

12. Cook with your child. Following directions, measuring, sorting ingredients, and managing time are all key elements to developing great organizational skills.

"There's a home for everything! Every whatchamacallit has its own spot. When you take something out, just put it back. Being organized really does ROCK!"